*The Berenstain Bears*

# READY, GET SET, GO!

We all have something
we do the best —
a little bit better
than the rest.

# GET SET, GO!

## Stan & Jan Berenstain

Random House New York

Copyright ©1988 by Berenstains, Inc. All rights reserved under International and Pan-American Copyright Conventions. Published in the United States by Random House, Inc., New York, and simultaneously in Canada by Random House of Canada Limited, Toronto.

*Library of Congress Cataloging-in-Publication Data:*
Berenstain, Stan. The Berenstain bears ready, get set, go! (A first time reader) SUMMARY: The Bear family engage in competitive sports events while demonstrating to the reader the comparison of adjectives. [1. Bears—Fiction. 2. Sports—Fiction. 3. Stories in rhyme] I. Berenstain, Jan. II. Title. III. Series: Berenstain, Stan. First time reader. PZ8.3.B4493Bhc 1988 [E] 88-42589 ISBN: 0-394-80564-X (pbk.); 0-394-90564-4 (lib. bdg.)

Manufactured in the United States of America      3 4 5 6 7 8 9 0

"Hooray! Hooray!"
their friends all say.
"The Bears' Olympics
start today!"

Ready, get set, run!

Papa runs fast.

Brother runs faster.

But Sister runs fastest.

Fast, faster, fastest.
Good, better, best.

When it comes to running,
Sister is better
than the rest.

Ready, get set, jump!

Papa jumps far.

Sister jumps farther.

Brother jumps farthest.

Far, farther, farthest.
Good, better, best.

When it comes to jumping,
Brother is best—
a better jumper
than the rest.

Ready, get set, climb!

Papa climbs high.

Brother climbs higher.

Sister climbs highest.

High, higher, highest.
Good, better, best.

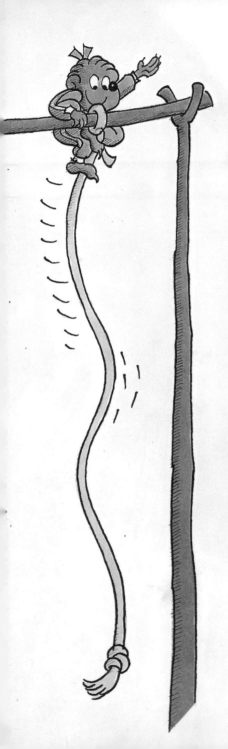

When it comes to climbing,
Sister is better
than the rest.

Poor old Papa.
Won't he EVER
do something the best?

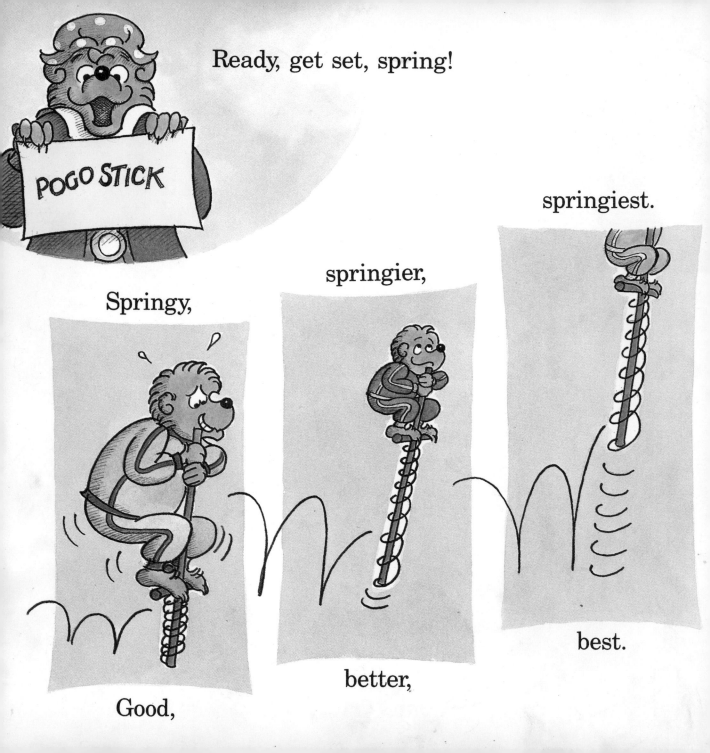

Papa, Brother, Sister,
all need a rest.

"Whew!" says Sister.
"Whew!" says Brother.
"Whew!" says Papa.

Poor old Papa.
Won't he EVER
do something the best —
much, much better
than the rest?

Ready, get set, sleep!

The Bears go to sleep.

Sister sleeps long.
She is a good sleeper.

Brother sleeps longer.
He is a better sleeper.

Papa's still asleep!
He is the best sleeper.

Long, longer,

Good, better,

longest.

best.

"Hooray! Hooray!"
their friends all shout.
"Without a doubt!
Without a doubt!
There IS something
Papa Bear does the best!
He's a much better sleeper
than the rest!"